AZTEC WARRIORS

by Valerie Bodden

Published by The Child's World
1980 Lookout Drive • Mankato, MN 56003-1705
800-599-READ • www.childsworld.com

ACKNOWLEDGMENTS
The Child's World: Mary Berendes, Publishing Director
Red Line Editorial: Editorial direction
The Design Lab: Design
Amnet: Production
Content Consultant: Arnaud F. Lambert, PhD, Associate
Professor of Anthropology, Onondaga Community College
Design elements: iStockphoto
Photographs ©: Dorling Kindersley/Thinkstock, cover, 16,
30 (top); Heritage Images/Corbis, 4; Bettmann/Corbis, 6,
12, 22; Public Domain, 7, 11,17, 21; Corbis, 9; Photos.com/
Thinkstock, 14; Mario Guzman/epa/Corbis, 18, 30 (center);
Gianni Dagli Orti/Corbis, 20; Gary Yim/Shutterstock, 24;
Lebrecht Music & Arts/Corbis, 26, 30 (bottom); Sergio
Dorantes/Corbis, 28

ISBN 9781631437540
LCCN 2014945424

Printed in the United States of America
Mankato, MN
November, 2014
PA02246

ABOUT THE AUTHOR

Valerie Bodden has written more than 200 nonfiction books for children. Her books have received positive reviews from School Library Journal, Booklist, Children's Literature, ForeWord Magazine, Horn Book Guide, VOYA, *and* Library Media Connection. *Bodden lives in Wisconsin with her husband and four young children.*

TABLE OF CONTENTS

Aztec warriors fought to defend their temple and city.

CHAPTER ONE

INTO BATTLE

The sounds of wooden drums, conch shell trumpets, and ceramic flutes filled the air. Thousands of men howled, whistled, and shouted along. The Aztec battle had begun.

One young Aztec man looked across the large, grassy battlefield. Beyond it he could see the enemy city. He had traveled to many battlefields before. But he had only carried supplies. Today he would finally join the fight.

The young man waited as the archers, spear throwers, and slingers hurled their weapons. Then he ran forward for hand-to-hand combat. He fought beside more experienced warriors. They could help him through his first battle. But he hoped he would not need their help. If he captured an enemy on his own, he would officially be a warrior. Someday, he might even reach the top ranks of the Aztec army. The more enemies he captured, the higher he could rise. But first he had to survive this battle.

Farmers and Fighters

Aztec battles involving large numbers of warriors usually took place during the late fall, winter, or early spring. The rest of the year, many Aztec warriors worked as farmers. They stayed home to tend their fields. Battles requiring fewer warriors could be fought any time of the year.

Aztec farmers grew maize and other crops.

ANOTHER VIEW
PAYING TRIBUTE

The people the Aztecs defeated were usually allowed to keep their own rulers and lands. But they had to pay **tribute** to the Aztecs. A **city-state** of the empire paid tribute with goods, services, or slaves. Some places had to send honey, grain, or cotton to the Aztec capital of Tenochtitlán. Others sent jewelry, warrior costumes, or feathers from tropical birds. Some city-states paid tribute by defending the Aztec Empire. How do you think people of the empire felt about paying tribute to the Aztec capital?

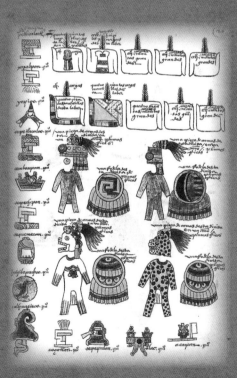

A record of the tribute owed by an Aztec city-state shows the goods paid, including warrior costumes.

CHAPTER TWO

RISE OF THE AZTEC WARRIOR

The Aztec people lived in the Valley of Mexico from the 1200s to the 1500s. Their capital city was Tenochtitlán. It was an island city in Lake Texcoco. The Aztecs started as a small group. They paid tribute to neighboring **allies**. Through war and **conquest**, the Aztecs grew into a vast empire. At its height in the early 1500s, the Aztec Empire included 6 million people. It stretched across present-day Mexico.

The Aztecs did not have a standing army of professional soldiers. Instead, all Aztec men marched to war when called upon by a ruler. The Aztecs could raise an army of 200,000 warriors if needed.

The mighty Aztec capital of Tenochtitlán, called Mexico
City by the Spanish, was built on a lake island.

A boy's training for military service started early. Young boys played with shields and spears. They played war games with their friends, too. When they were teenagers, the boys went to school.

The boys of **noble** families went to one type of school. They trained to become priests, government officials, or military leaders. They studied history and religion. They learned to read and write, too. Common boys went to another type of school. Like noble boys, they learned about history and religion. But they were not taught to read and write.

At both kinds of schools, the main focus was military training. Students practiced fighting skills. They learned to use weapons. They also did hard labor. They hauled wood, dug canals, and built walls. Once they had been trained, the boys served as wartime supply carriers. After that, they marched into battle. A warrior rose in rank by taking enemy captives.

The main reason the Aztecs went to war was to gain tribute and enemy captives. Tribute payments made

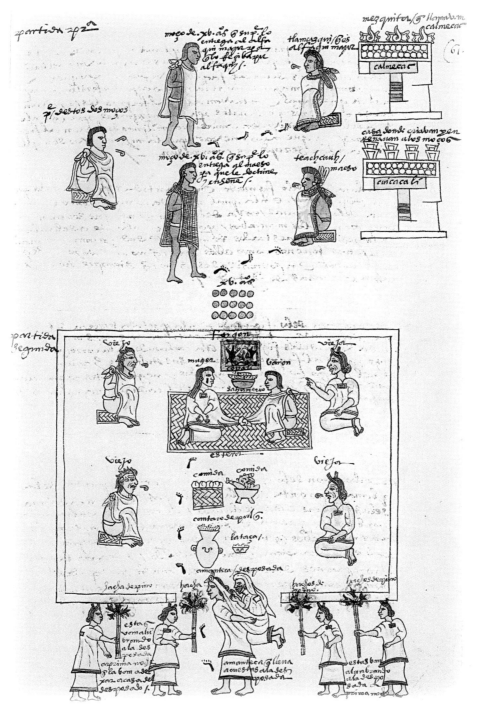

The *Codex Mendoza*, a book about Aztec life, shows
Aztec boys training for the military or priesthood
(top) and a girl getting married (bottom).

A captive's heart is offered to the Aztec gods.

the Aztec capital wealthy. Enemy captives were needed for religious ceremonies. The captives were killed as **sacrifices** to the Aztec gods. The Aztecs believed the gods needed blood as payment for creating the world. The Aztecs and their enemies sometimes arranged special wars known as flower wars. These wars were fought just to capture enemy warriors.

The Aztec Gods

The Aztec gods were an important part of war. Priests prayed to the gods to learn when to go to war. Priests also went with warriors to the battlefields. They carried images of the gods with them. After the war, captives were sacrificed to the gods.

ANOTHER VIEW
TOUGH TRAINING

While in school, Aztec boys faced many hardships. Some had to sleep on the bare stone floor. They had little clothing and often had to go without food. Boys were sometimes woken up in the middle of the night to do dangerous jobs. During the day, the boys practiced fighting skills and did hard physical work. This training was meant to teach future warriors self-discipline and courage. How do you think Aztec boys felt about becoming warriors?

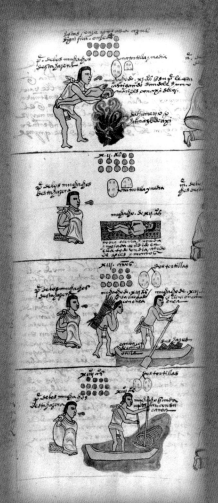

Aztec boys had to learn many skills to become warriors.

CHAPTER THREE

CLOTHING AND WEAPONS

An Aztec warrior's clothing was based on his rank or experience. A new warrior might wear only a **loincloth** and a plain cloak. He had a long lock of hair at the back of his head. This showed that he had not yet taken a captive. When a warrior took his first captive, the lock was cut. He also received a cape. He was allowed to paint his face.

After he took a second captive, the warrior could wear sandals in battle. He also received a new cape and a bodysuit decorated with red feathers. The highest officers often had costumes completely covered with feathers

and other decorations.
They wore wooden helmets
shaped like monkeys,
parrots, eagles, or other
animals. But it was difficult
to move around in these
costumes. The costumes also
made the officers targets.
Capturing a high-ranking
Aztec warrior brought great
honor to enemy soldiers.

Under their costumes,
most warriors wore suits of
quilted cotton. The thick
cotton easily stopped
stone-tipped arrows and
darts. Many warriors
carried shields made of animal

A warrior without much
experience wore simple
clothing, including a loincloth.

hides, woven palm leaves, or wood. A low-ranking
warrior carried a plain shield. But high-ranking
officers used shields covered with feathers, gold, or
turquoise tiles.

Sharp blades like teeth lined clubs used by Aztec warriors.

Aztec warriors used a variety of weapons. Their main weapon was a sword called a *maquahuitl*. The sword was a little longer than 3 feet (1 m). It was made of a long, flat piece of wood lined with short obsidian teeth. Obsidian is a hard rock formed from cooled lava. These teeth made the sword sharp enough to cut off a horse's head. Long thrusting spears had similar blades. Warriors also carried clubs or copper axes. Slings were used for throwing stones. Some warriors used bows and arrows. Others carried spear-throwers called *atlatls*. They launched spears with enough force to pierce metal armor.

Jaguar and Eagle Warriors

The Jaguar and Eagle warriors were very high in rank. They had taken more than four captives. In battle, a Jaguar warrior wore a jaguar-skin costume. The head of the jaguar was the helmet. The warrior's head stuck out from the animal's mouth. An Eagle warrior wore a large helmet shaped like an eagle's head. The warrior's head came up through the eagle's beak. Jaguar and Eagle warriors received other honors, too. They could eat at the emperor's palace.

An Eagle warrior statue stood near the main temple at Tenochtitlán.

Another View
Women and War

Aztec women did not serve as warriors. But women did have roles to play in an Aztec war. They prepared food and supplies for the army. If their home or family was in danger, they defended it. Women were sometimes taken captive or offered as tribute. In addition, many women became widows as a result of war. But if a woman's husband survived, he would earn rewards and honor for their family. How do you think women felt when they learned there would soon be a war?

CHAPTER FOUR

BATTLE TACTICS

The Aztecs did not launch surprise attacks. Instead, they sent messengers to the city-state they wanted to conquer. The messengers demanded that the city-state pay tribute to the Aztecs. If the people agreed, they were spared from fighting. But if they refused, the Aztecs declared war. The Aztecs met with the leader of the city-state to choose a place and time for the battle.

Wars were also declared if the Aztecs had been insulted. An attack on an Aztec merchant visiting another city-state was considered an insult. If the Aztecs really wanted to go to war, they might hire a merchant to provoke such an attack. During times of peace, flower wars were arranged between rulers. The wars allowed warriors to capture victims for sacrifices.

Aztec artists carved images of battling warriors in stone.

Aztec warriors fought for the emperor, who sometimes marched into battle with them. To reach some battles, the warriors marched hundreds of miles. When they arrived, the warriors lined up across from the enemy army on the battlefield. Warriors on both sides beat drums, blew trumpets, and shook rattles. The instruments relayed messages during the battle.

Aztec warriors burned down a town's temple after winning a battle.

The two sides advanced. They stopped when they were nearly 200 feet (60 m) apart. Then archers shot arrows into the enemy lines. Slingers hurled stones from their slingshots. After they ran out of arrows and stones, the warriors moved to the back of the battle lines. The two armies advanced again. This time, warriors launched their spears.

When the spears were gone, the warriors rushed toward the enemy's line to attack. They slashed the

Musicians played for the returning warriors after a battle win.

enemy with their swords. As the warriors got tired, new warriors from the rear took their places. The most experienced warriors fought at the front of the battle lines. Some of these warriors vowed never to retreat. Newer warriors stayed near the rear of the group. Many warriors on both sides died. But the Aztecs tried to weaken some enemy warriors by cutting through their muscles and bones with their swords. That way the enemy warriors could be captured alive.

Battles ended when one side surrendered or retreated. If the Aztecs won the battle, they burned down the enemy's temple. They made the people pay tribute to the Aztec capital. But they usually did not destroy the enemy's city or harm the remaining people.

After battle, the Aztec warriors returned home. If they had won, they were greeted with the playing of drums and trumpets. They received capes, chocolate, and lip plugs as rewards. If they had lost, the priests wept. The surviving warriors returned in tears, too. They also burned their weapons.

DIFFERENT TACTICS

The Aztecs used many different battle tactics. Before a war, they often sent spies to the enemy city. The spies gathered information about the enemy's forces. In battle, the Aztecs sometimes pretended to retreat. When the enemy followed, the Aztecs launched an **ambush**. Aztec warriors also tried to make their enemies panic. The Aztecs would completely surround the enemy army. This left only a small opening for escape. It was hard for enemy warriors to get through the opening without being attacked.

ANOTHER VIEW
SACRIFICIAL VICTIMS

Many captives were treated as slaves. But some captives of the Aztecs were treated well. They were reserved for special rituals. Their injuries were treated and they were fed fine foods. But the captives knew they would soon be sacrificed. A captive's chest was cut open. The captive's heart was ripped out. Afterward, the captive's head might be stuck on a skull rack. How do you think captives felt as they waited to be sacrificed?

A carved skull rack was found in the ruins of the main temple at Tenochtitlán.

CHAPTER FIVE

THE SPANISH CONQUEST

When the Aztecs first settled in Tenochtitlán in 1325, they were not very strong. They made an **alliance** with the Tepanecs. The Tepanecs were another group of people living in the Valley of Mexico. The Aztecs paid tribute to the Tepanecs and fought for them. But in 1428, the Aztecs defeated the Tepanecs. After that, the Tepanecs paid tribute to the Aztecs.

The Aztec ruler Montezuma I took the throne in 1440. He launched battles to expand Aztec control. During his rule, the Aztecs gathered an army of 200,000 warriors. In 1458, the army fought the Mixtec and Zapotec peoples. The Aztecs continued to fight until nearly all of the enemy soldiers had been killed or captured.

Montezuma II ruled the Aztecs during the height of the empire.

After Montezuma I's rule ended, the Tarascan army defeated the Aztecs in 1478. In 1502, Montezuma II took the throne. He continued to battle the Tarascans without success.

In 1519, Spanish soldier and explorer Hernán Cortés arrived in Mexico. He had 500 soldiers with him. Montezuma II sent Cortés many gifts to show the Aztecs' power. He thought this power would scare the

Spanish away. But the gifts made Cortés want to come to Tenochtitlán.

When Cortés arrived in the city, Montezuma II welcomed him. But Cortés soon took Montezuma II captive. In May 1520, Spanish troops killed many Aztecs during a religious ceremony. Fighting broke out and thousands of Aztecs were killed. Soon after, Montezuma II was killed.

By June, the Spanish had suffered heavy losses. They fled the city. The Aztecs thought the fight was over. They did not follow the Spanish troops. But several months later, the Spanish marched back to Tenochtitlán. Along the way, the Spanish asked native peoples to fight with them against the Aztecs. More than 70,000 native warriors agreed. With the Spanish, they laid **siege** to Tenochtitlán. The siege lasted several months.

Aztec warriors continued to fight, but they were weak. The Spanish blocked deliveries of food into the city. Many people starved. In addition, many Aztecs had fallen ill with smallpox. This deadly disease spread from the Spanish. On August 13, 1521, the Spanish captured Cuauhtémoc, the new Aztec emperor. The war was over. The Aztec Empire had come to an end.

Mexican artist Diego Rivera's mural shows the
Spanish battling Aztec warriors.

In its place, the Spanish formed the empire of
New Spain. They built their new capital of Mexico
City on top of the ruins of Tenochtitlán. The mighty
Aztec warriors gradually faded into the past with their
empire. But during their short history, Aztec warriors
were brave and fierce fighters.

Tenochtitlán

The island capital of Tenochtitlán was connected to the mainland by several **causeways**. Floating gardens and farming plots surrounded the city. Broad roads and canals crossed the island. They led to the city's center, where temples stood atop step pyramids. The city center also included huge stone palaces for the emperor, surrounded by gardens and ponds.

Another View
Amazed and horrified

The Spanish soldiers were awed by the city of Tenochtitlán. With 200,000 people, it was bigger than most cities in Europe. Some thought it looked like a dream or a vision. At the same time, the Spanish were horrified by the Aztec practice of human sacrifice. How do you think the soldiers felt as they went to war against the Aztecs?

TIMELINE

1325
The Aztecs settle in Tenochtitlán.

1440
Montezuma I becomes Aztec emperor.

1458
The Aztecs battle the Mixtec and Zapotec peoples.

1502
Montezuma II becomes Aztec emperor.

1519
Hernán Cortés lands in the Aztec Empire.

1520
Montezuma II is killed.

1521
The Spanish defeat the Aztecs.

GLOSSARY

alliance (uh-LYE-unss) An alliance is an agreement to work together peacefully. The Aztecs made an alliance with the Tepanecs.

allies (AL-lyes) Allies are people or groups who join together for a common purpose, such as fighting a war. The early Aztecs paid tribute to their allies.

ambush (AM-bush) An ambush is when one group hides and then attacks another group by surprise. An ambush was a battle tactic used by the Aztecs.

causeways (KAWZ-wayz) Causeways are raised roads built across water or low ground. Several causeways linked Tenochtitlán with the mainland.

city-state (SIT-ee-stayt) A city-state is part of an empire with a central city and surrounding area. A city-state paid tribute to the Aztec capital.

conquest (KON-kwest) A conquest is the act of defeating and taking control of an enemy. The Spanish conquest ended the Aztec Empire.

loincloth (LOYN-kloth) A loincloth is a piece of cloth worn over the lower torso to cover private areas of the body. A new Aztec warrior wore a simple loincloth.

noble (NOH-buhl) A noble is a person from an important or ruling family. Noble Aztec children went to different schools than common children.

sacrifices (SAK-ruh-fis-ses) Sacrifices are offerings made to gods. Human captives were used as sacrifices to the Aztec gods.

siege (SEEJ) A siege is when troops surround a city or other area to cause its people to surrender. The Spanish laid siege to the Aztec capital.

tribute (TRIB-yoot) A tribute is a rent or tax paid by subjects to their ruler. A city-state's tribute was paid in goods or services.

TO LEARN MORE

BOOKS

Dwyer, Helen, and Mary A. Stout. *Aztec History and Culture*.
New York: Gareth Stevens, 2013.

Macdonald, Fiona. *An Aztec Warrior*.
Mankato, MN: Book House, 2015.

Wood, Alix. *Human Sacrifice*.
New York: Gareth Stevens, 2014.

WEB SITES

Visit our Web site for links about Aztec warriors:
childsworld.com/links

Note to Parents, Teachers, and Librarians: We routinely verify our Web links to make sure they are safe and active sites. So encourage your readers to check them out!

INDEX